NEVADA

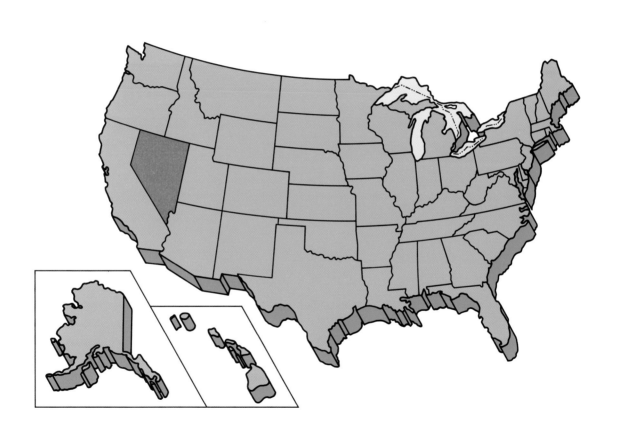

Hello U★S★A★

NEVADA

Karen Sirvaitis

Lerner Publications Company

Cover photograph courtesy of Circus Circus Hotel/Casino-Las Vegas, Pro Process-Pro Display.

The glossary that begins on page 68 gives definitions of words shown in **bold type** in the text.

LIBRARY OF CONGRESS
CATALOGING-IN-PUBLICATION DATA
Sirvaitis, Karen.
    Nevada / Karen Sirvaitis.
      p.   cm. — (Hello USA)
    Includes index.
    Summary: An introduction to the geography, history, economy, people, environmental issues, and interesting sites of Nevada.
    ISBN 0-8225-2719-7 (lib. bdg.)
    1. Nevada—Juvenile literature.
[1. Nevada.] I. Title. II. Series.
F841.3.S57 1992
979.3—dc20   91-20624
                  CIP
                  AC

Manufactured in the United States of America
1 2 3 4 5 6 7 8 9 10 01 00 99 98 97 96 95 94 93 92

 This book is printed on acid-free, recyclable paper.

CONTENTS

Did You Know . . . ?

❏ The last great western bank robbery was staged in Winnemucca, Nevada, on September 19, 1900. Butch Cassidy and the Wild Bunch crept into town and made off with more than $32,000 from the First National Bank. The gang escaped to Wyoming on stolen horses.

❏ One of Nevada's mining towns, Virginia City, was once so rich that its streets were paved with silver.

❑ Nevada's first speed limit was set in Tonopah in 1905. Cars in the town were not allowed to go faster than 4 miles (6.4 kilometers) per hour—the speed of a brisk walk.

❑ Some of the world's largest ichthyosaur fossils have been found near Berlin, Nevada. The prehistoric reptiles grew up to 60 feet (18 meters) long and 8 feet (2 m) around.

❑ The oldest living trees in the world—Great Basin bristlecone pine trees—are found in Nevada. Some of the evergreens are more than 4,000 years old!

Great Basin bristlecone pine tree

7

A Trip
Around the State

Colorful rocks, darting lizards, and prickly cactuses are only a few of the many images of Nevada. Within this landscape and beyond, Nevada is full of surprises and wonders.

8

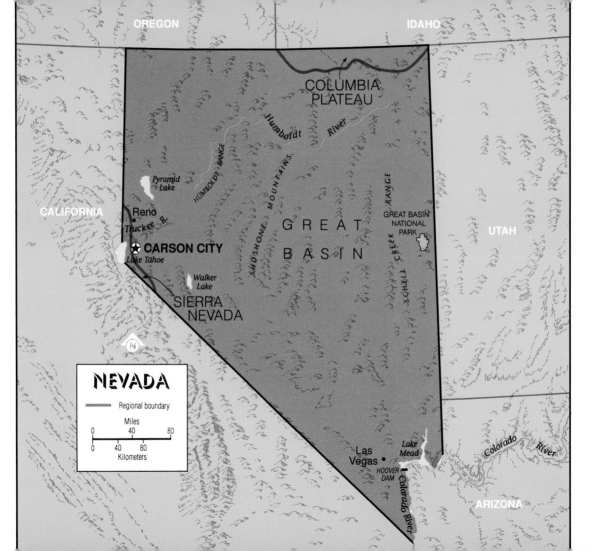

OREGON

IDAHO

COLUMBIA
PLATEAU

Humboldt   *River*

HUMBOLDT RANGE

Pyramid
Lake

CALIFORNIA

Reno
Truckee R.

CARSON CITY

Lake Tahoe

*Walker
Lake*

SIERRA
NEVADA

GREAT
BASIN

SHOSHONE MOUNTAINS

SCHELL CREEK RANGE

SNAKE RANGE

GREAT BASIN
NATIONAL
PARK

UTAH

Las
Vegas

Lake
Mead

Colorado   *River*

*HOOVER
DAM*

Colorado River

ARIZONA

NEVADA

━━━━ Regional boundary

Miles
0   40   80

0   40   80
Kilometers

Nevada, the seventh largest state in the country, is part of the Rocky Mountain region of the western United States. The state is bordered by Oregon, Idaho, Utah, Arizona, and California. Like its five neighbors, Nevada has deserts, mountains, pine trees, and lakes.

Nevada is divided into three land regions. The Great Basin covers most of the state. Nevada's other regions—the Columbia Plateau and the Sierra Nevada—are much smaller than the Great Basin but add striking features to the landscape.

Much of the Great Basin is **desert,** or dry land, and mountain ranges. Nevada's Great Basin is part of a much larger region that spans several states. The basin is shaped somewhat like a large, shallow bowl—that is, the region is higher around the edges and lower in the center. As a result, many of the Great Basin's rivers drain inward instead of up and out toward the sea.

Desert shrubs and grasses cover parts of the Great Basin.

Pine-covered mountains jut up from Nevada's desert scenery.

Humboldt, Shoshone, and Schell Creek are among the Great Basin's largest mountain ranges. Pine trees blanket some of the slopes. **Mesas,** or flat-topped hills, and valleys separate the ranges.

The Columbia Plateau region of northeastern Nevada lies on top of hardened **lava.** Thousands of years ago, hot, liquid lava, or melted rock, seeped up from deep within the earth's crust and spread over the land. As it cooled, the lava turned into rock, creating a **plateau,** or flat highland. Over thousands of years, rivers cut deep gorges into the plateau, forming canyons.

The Sierra Nevada is a mountain range extending 400 miles (644 km) north to south along part of eastern California. A short stretch of the mountains crosses into western Nevada, forming the state's third region. A few lakes dot Nevada's Sierra Nevada region. Lake Tahoe, a popular vacation spot, straddles Nevada's border with California.

About one-tenth of Nevada was once buried under a gigantic lake called Lahontan. Over thousands of years, Lahontan dried up almost completely, leaving only the much smaller Pyramid and Walker lakes in western Nevada. Pyramid is the one lake in the world to harbor the ancient cui-ui, a type of fish that has managed to survive many changes in its environment.

Lake Tahoe is 22 miles (35 km) long and 1,685 feet (514 m) deep.

The Hoover Dam is one of the world's tallest concrete dams.

Lake Mead is Nevada's largest **reservoir,** or artificial lake. At 227 square miles (588 sq km), Lake Mead is also one of the largest reservoirs in the world. The lake was created when workers built the Hoover Dam in 1936 to control the flow of the Colorado River in southeastern Nevada.

The Colorado River defines most of Nevada's border with Arizona. Some other major waterways in the state include the Truckee and Humboldt rivers. The Truckee winds from Lake Tahoe down into Pyramid Lake. Farther north the Humboldt River flows west into Humboldt Lake.

Seasons and temperatures vary in Nevada. Southern Nevada has long, hot summers and short, mild winters. Summer temperatures average 80° F (27° C), with daytime temperatures often above 100° F (38° C). Winter temperatures seldom drop below freezing (32° F/ 0° C). In the northern part of the state, summers are also hot, but winters bring temperatures from 10° F to 36° F (–12° C to 2 °C).

Most of the state gets very little snow, but each year the Sierra Nevada receives up to 24 inches (61 centimeters). In Spanish, the word *nevada* means "snow-clad." Nevada takes its name from these mountains.

Nevada is the driest of the 50 states. An average of only 9 inches (23 cm) of rain and snow falls in

Nevada takes its name from the snow-covered Sierra Nevada mountains.

Nevada each year. Because the state can get so dry and hot, some bodies of water in Nevada—including Humboldt Lake and part of the Humboldt River—dry up during the summer.

A wild burro makes its home in Rhyolite, a ghost town in central Nevada.

When rain does appear, it is sometimes dramatic, causing a **flash flood**. This usually happens once or twice a year, when a brief thunderstorm pounds the desert. Rushing rainwater carries sand downhill, forming a channel. As the channel widens, more water travels faster and faster, washing away almost everything in its path.

The amount of rain that falls in the desert can support only the hardiest of plants. Sagebrush, which smells of sweet sage but tastes bitter, needs little water to survive. This bushy plant thrives in the state's deserts, earning Nevada one of its nicknames—the Sagebrush State. Desert conditions are also ideal for cactuses, which are able to store water in their stems.

Forests of aspen and pine cover Nevada's mountainsides. Willows and cottonwoods line riverbanks. Wildflowers, such as the Indian paintbrush and the violet, bloom in the state's meadows during the spring.

Large animals found in Nevada include mule deer, pronghorn antelope, and bighorn sheep. The sure-footed bighorn lives high in the mountains, where its enemies find the steep slopes too dangerous to tread. Bands of wild horses and of burros run throughout the state, while badgers and porcupines scuttle about. Nevada's lakes and rivers carry an abundance of trout and bass.

The mountain bluebird is Nevada's state bird.

Crossing Nevada's Great Basin was a dangerous undertaking for early explorers.

Nevada's Story

"Beyond this place there be dragons." That's how mapmakers first described Nevada's Great Basin. Crossing the dry, sun-scorched desert meant certain death for anyone who dared try. These explorers did not know how to find food and water in the desert. But they would learn from the Indians, as the Indians had learned from their ancestors.

The first peoples to enter the Great Basin probably arrived about 12,000 years ago. These Native Americans gathered seeds and roots for food. They used spears to hunt animals. By about A.D. 100, the Indians had begun to grow some of their food near rivers, using tools to plant crops.

Indian paintbrush

19

These farming Indians became known as the Basket Makers because they made baskets and other items from dried grasses. The Basket Makers wove their containers tight enough to hold water. By placing a few sunbaked rocks, seeds, and water into a basket, the Indians made a hot soup.

Around the year 750, the Basket Makers discovered how to channel water from rivers and streams to their crops. This process, called **irrigation**, was important for Indians trying to survive in the dry Great Basin. With well-watered crops, the Basket Makers could grow a lot of food.

Their harvests were plentiful, and the Basket Makers no longer needed to move around the region searching for food. Using clay, they built flat-roofed houses called **pueblos.** The Basket Makers who lived in these homes eventually became known as the Pueblo Indians.

Pueblo Indians dance to celebrate their harvest.

In what is now the southeastern corner of Nevada, the Pueblo Indians built a large city known as Pueblo Grande de Nevada. At one time, the community may have had as many as 20,000 residents. People farmed, hunted, mined, and traded with other Indian groups.

Pueblo Grande is also known as the Lost City, and it could be called Nevada's first **ghost town.** No one really knows why, but the Pueblo Indians had abandoned the city and the rest of the Great Basin by the year 1150.

At about the same time, other Indians were moving into the Great Basin. The largest tribes

This pueblo is part of the ancient Indian city of Pueblo Grande de Nevada.

were the Shoshone, the Paiute, and the Washo. Unlike the Pueblo Indians, the newcomers moved from place to place, hunting animals and gathering most of their foods from the wild.

Because they moved often, these Indians built temporary shelters. Each family took care of its own needs, making sure to have enough food and clothing for itself. Small villages existed, and each had a leader. The village leader sometimes organized rabbit and antelope hunts, or the yearly harvest of pine nuts, but had little control over the daily lives of the people.

Indians living in the deserts of the Great Basin spent most of their time finding food. They probably had little contact with explorers and fur trappers who began to arrive in the area from Britain and the United States in the early 1800s. At that time, the United States was a new nation whose borders were on the eastern coast of North America.

In 1826 Peter Skene Ogden of the Hudson's Bay Company entered what is now northeastern Nevada. The same year, Jedediah Strong Smith of the Rocky Mountain Fur Company followed the Colorado River into southern Nevada. Both men were looking for something worth a lot of money—beavers.

During the 1800s, beavers were probably the most hunted animals in North America. A beaver pelt *(above)* was soft and could be sewn into a fashionable hat or coat.

Fur trappers in North America often got rich selling pelts to customers in Europe and Asia, where beaver hats were popular. Searching for beavers, Ogden and Smith led their tired and hungry parties through mountain snowstorms and across blistering deserts in what is now Nevada.

In the years to come, Smith and Ogden returned to Nevada. They brought other fur trappers and befriended the Indians, who helped the newcomers find food and water in the desert. Smith and Ogden did not find as many beavers as they had hoped to, and few people came to the Great Basin.

But something happened in 1848 that caused more than 30,000 people to brave Nevada's deserts and mountains—the California gold rush.

To reach the gold in California, miners crossed the Great Basin on trails that had been mapped out by Smith, Ogden, and other explorers. Many travelers followed the Humboldt River. Some of these people chose to stay in Nevada. Most of

During the 1850s, miners bought supplies at the Mormon trading post in Genoa.

those who remained were Mormons, or members of the Church of Jesus Christ of Latter-day Saints.

In 1850 the Mormons set up a trading post near the California-Nevada border and sold supplies to traveling miners. These Mormons built homes and planted and irrigated crops. Non-Mormons also came to live near the trading post.

It grew into Genoa, the first town settled by white people in Nevada.

The Mormons left Genoa in 1857. That year church leaders called all Mormons to Salt Lake City, Utah, to fight in the Mormon War. Only about 1,000 settlers remained in Nevada in 1859, when two miners discovered silver and gold in western Nevada.

The discovery, named the Comstock Lode, lured thousands of fortune seekers to the mines. The rich deposits of silver made some people millionaires. Others unknowingly sold their mining claims for much less than they were worth, while still others lost their fortunes in poker games or to thieves.

Wealthy miners built Silver City, Gold Hill, and Virginia City. With thousands of residents, Virginia City quickly became the largest and busiest town in Nevada. It boasted mansions, first-class hotels, 110 saloons, and the *Territorial Enterprise,* the newspaper on which the writer Mark Twain began his career.

The Comstock Lode *(above)* drew thousands of miners to western Nevada in the 1860s. At first they lived in tents or stone huts. But before long, the miners had built several towns. The largest town was Virginia City *(left)*.

In 1861, the year the Northern and Southern states began fighting each other in the Civil War, the U.S. government created the Nevada Territory. Abraham Lincoln, the president of the United States, wanted Nevada to become a state. Most Nevadans supported Lincoln and the Union, or Northern states.

By making Nevada a state, Lincoln could use its silver and gold to pay the Union's war costs. He could also keep Nevada's valuable minerals out of enemy hands.

But there was a problem. To become a state, a territory had to have at least 127,381 people. Nevada had less than 20,000.

Despite the territory's low population, Nevadans drew up a state

People going to Nevada in the 1800s sometimes traveled by stagecoach.

Sprigs of sagebrush, the state flower, form a wreath on Nevada's flag. The silver star symbolizes Nevada's mineral wealth, and the words "Battle Born" indicate that Nevada became a state during the Civil War.

constitution. On October 31, 1864, the U.S. government made an exception and allowed Nevada to join the Union as the 36th state. Because it was admitted during the Civil War, Nevada has since been called the Battle Born State.

As Nevada's population grew, the area's Indians were slowly forced off their homelands. Some bands of Paiute, Shoshone, and Washo became hostile. They attacked miners and other settlers who had invaded Indian land.

On reservations, Native Americans often lived in poverty.

In the 1870s, lawmakers decided that Indians and settlers could not live side by side peacefully. The U.S. government set up areas of land called **reservations,** on which the Indians could live without fear of losing their land to newcomers. The Indians were expected to stay on this land and to grow their own food. But they were used to their freedom. The Indians had a hard time living on reservations.

Mining in Nevada reached its peak during the 1870s. Nearly 30,000 people lived in Virginia City alone. But by the end of the decade, the U.S. government had begun to pay less money for silver. Mining in Nevada was no longer profitable.

Miners pose in front of a mine at Pickhandle Gulch.

Large areas of grassland attracted Basques *(opposite page)* **to Nevada to herd sheep** *(above).*

Tens of thousands of people left the state. Nevada's population dropped by almost half. Some cities were completely abandoned, turning into ghost towns overnight.

Many of those who stayed in Nevada started raising beef cattle. Others, mostly Basques (people from a region in Spain), settled in northern Nevada in the 1880s to herd sheep on the grasslands.

Livestock ranching, however, was not nearly as profitable as mining silver or gold had been. Times were difficult for Nevada's ranchers, who paid high rates to ship their meat and wool by train to markets in the eastern United States.

Nevadans soon discovered that the Comstock Lode was not the only source of minerals in their state. In the early 1900s, prospectors found more deposits of gold, silver, and copper, and Nevada experienced another mining boom.

Probably just as important as

Silver was discovered in 1900 at Tonopah.

minerals to Nevadans was the completion of the Newlands Irrigation Project in 1907. The project, a system of dams built on the Truckee and Carson rivers, stored water needed for irrigation. With a reliable source of water, farmers could grow more crops.

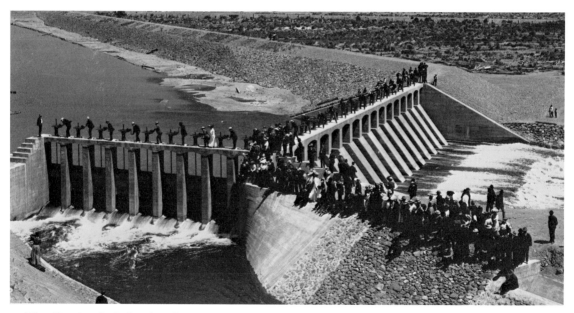

The Newlands Irrigation Project, built near the town of Reno, helped Nevada's farmers irrigate their crops.

People crowded the casinos in the 1930s, when gambling in Nevada became legal again.

Throughout most of Nevada's mining days, **gambling,** or betting money on various games, had been popular. The practice was outlawed in 1910. But in 1931, the state government again legalized gambling throughout Nevada—the only state at the time to have done so. Reno and other towns reopened their old gambling houses, called **casinos.** Once again, people were coming to Nevada to try and strike it rich.

In 1936 workers finished the Hoover Dam, one of the largest dams in the world. Located on the Colorado River, the Hoover Dam stored water for irrigation, households, and businesses. The dam also used waterpower to generate electricity. Because the Hoover Dam provided these services, surrounding communities, such as Las Vegas, could grow.

36

Construction of the Hoover Dam took six years.

In the 1950s, Nevadans could see giant clouds as they watched the testing of atomic bombs.

In 1950 about 160,000 people lived in Nevada, but much of the state was thinly populated. Partly for this reason, the U.S. government chose Nevada as a testing site for atomic bombs for use in warfare. Testing was needed to make sure the bombs worked and to study the effects of the explosions. Exploding bombs created mushroom-shaped clouds that could be seen for miles around.

People soon became afraid of the harmful effects of atomic bombs on people and the environment. In 1963 the tests were moved underground, where the effects of the explosions were not as great and could be more easily measured. The government continues to test atomic devices underground. In fact, the largest atomic testing site in the country is located in Nevada.

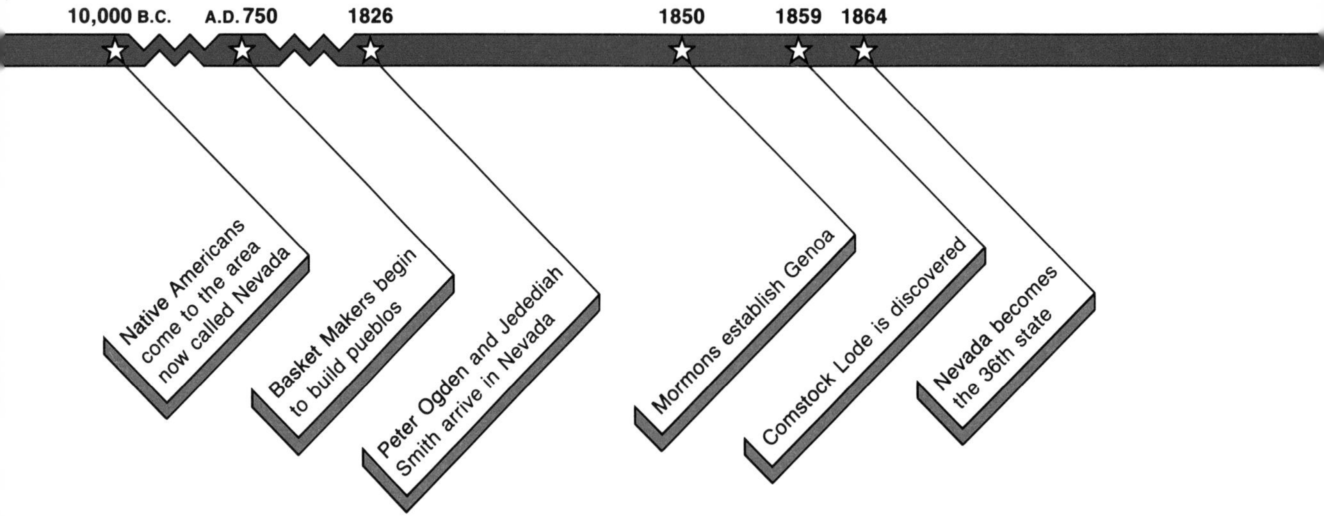

10,000 B.C.
A.D. 750
1826
1850
1859
1864
Native Americans come to the area now called Nevada
Basket Makers begin to build pueblos
Peter Ogden and Jedediah Smith arrive in Nevada
Mormons establish Genoa
Comstock Lode is discovered
Nevada becomes the 36th state

People are still concerned about the harmful effects of the underground bombs. For many people, the "dragons" feared by Nevada's first mapmakers no longer exist on the desert. They now breathe fire below the Great Basin. But Nevadans handled the desert, and they hope to overcome the challenges facing them now as well.

| 1907 | 1931 | 1936 | 1950 | 1990 |

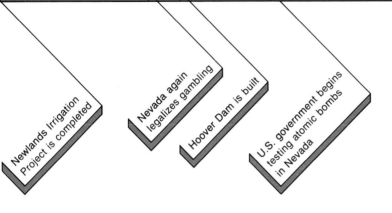

Newlands Irrigation Project is completed

Nevada again legalizes gambling

Hoover Dam is built

U.S. government begins testing atomic bombs in Nevada

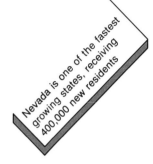

Nevada is one of the fastest growing states, receiving 400,000 new residents

Nevada's population is small but fast-growing. Between 1980 and 1990, Nevada gained over 400,000 new residents.

An elegant house built in Virginia City in 1868 is a reminder of Nevada's mining wealth. By the mid-1870s, nearly 20,000 people had moved to Virginia City to try and strike it rich.

Living and Working in Nevada

Silent saloons. Crumbling buildings. Long-deserted mines emptied of their treasures. Nevada's mining history lingers in the hundreds of ghost towns and abandoned mines located throughout the state. These towns are empty because most miners left once they had made their fortunes.

Many of Nevada's smaller towns actually had more people during the 1800s or early 1900s than they have today. Virginia City, once the state's largest mining town, is now a tourist attraction with only 800 residents. Tonopah, a mining town that once reached a population of 20,000, now has only 4,000 people.

Rochester, once a booming mining city, is now a ghost town.

The true ghost towns of Nevada are those without any residents. Rhyolite, Hamilton, Delamar, and Tybo are just a few of the many deserted mining areas in Nevada. Visitors can imagine decorated storefronts and noisy saloons, hear the sound of horses' hooves, and picture the miners heading out to their claims with picks in hand and burros in tow.

The people of Nevada's past came from many countries, but most present-day Nevadans are descendants of the British. Many of the recent **immigrants** come from Mexico, although a variety of foreign accents can be heard in the state. A number of Nevada's 15,000 Native Americans live on the state's 24 Indian reservations. African Americans make up 6 percent of the population.

Basque dancers

Paiute children play at the Pyramid Lake Reservation.

45

Nevada's capitol building is in Carson City.

All of these people totaled 1.2 million in the early 1990s. Las Vegas, the state's largest city, has about 260,000 residents and more jobs than any other town in Nevada. Reno is the second biggest, with nearly 135,000 people. Carson City, Nevada's capital, is home to about 40,000. Only 15 percent of the state's population lives in **rural** areas.

Compared to other states, Nevada has a small permanent population. But when you add the number of visitors who arrive on any given day, Nevada's population can double in size.

Gambling attracts the majority of visitors to Nevada. In Las Vegas, brightly lit casinos line Las Vegas Boulevard, better known as the Strip. People try their luck 24 hours a day at blackjack, poker, keno, slot machines, and more. Nightclubs advertise dozens of concerts and shows. The cities of Reno, Elko, and Laughlin are also popular choices for gaming and other entertainment.

At a Las Vegas resort, an acrobat balances on a high wire.

Visitors can view ancient rock drawings at Valley of Fire State Park.

Nevada also features several unique museums. The Liberace Museum in Las Vegas honors the piano player Liberace, who was a major attraction on the Strip during his lifetime. The musician's 75-foot-long (23-m-long) fox-skin cape and a 50-pound (23-kilogram) rhinestone are among his many belongings on display.

History buffs can visit the Old Mormon Fort. Built in 1855 by Mormons, the fort is the oldest building in Las Vegas. In Overton, the Lost City Museum displays tools and pottery found at Pueblo Grande de Nevada. The Nevada State Museum in Carson City features an underground mine that tourists can explore.

The U.S. government owns most of the land in Nevada—about 85 percent of it. But the government only recently established the state's first national park. Great Basin National Park in eastern Nevada boasts ancient bristlecone pine trees, deep caverns, the state's highest mountain peak, and miles and miles of lonesome trails.

Bristlecone pines line a trail in Great Basin National Park.

Skiers riding a chair lift have a spectacular view of Lake Tahoe *(right)*. At Pyramid Lake *(below)*, fishers inspect their catch.

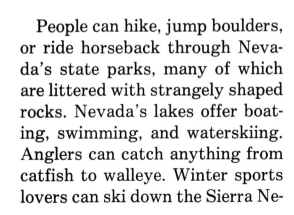

People can hike, jump boulders, or ride horseback through Nevada's state parks, many of which are littered with strangely shaped rocks. Nevada's lakes offer boating, swimming, and waterskiing. Anglers can catch anything from catfish to walleye. Winter sports lovers can ski down the Sierra Nevada or ice-skate near the resorts of Lake Tahoe.

Nearly 90 percent of Nevada's workers have jobs that help visitors and Nevadans alike. These workers have what are called service jobs. Hotel desk clerks, teachers, and the governor all have service jobs. Nellis Air Force Base in southern Nevada employs more than 10,000 service workers.

Manufacturing is the next biggest employer in Nevada, although factory workers make up only 5 percent of the work force. Computers, medical equipment, lumber products, neon signs, and pet food are among the many products made in the state. Las Vegas and Reno have the largest number of manufacturing plants in Nevada.

A pilot from Nevada flies over Las Vegas.

Mining is not as big an industry as it was in the 1870s, when Nevada earned the nickname the Silver State. But Nevada produces more gold, mercury, and magnesite than any other state in the country. Silver is still taken from the land, but gold now earns more money for the state. In northern Nevada, rigs drill for oil.

At a mine in northeastern Nevada, gold is separated from ore.

Livestock ranching has been successful in Nevada since the 1880s. Cattle and sheep graze on more than 50 million acres (20 million hectares). Because of the small amount of rain in Nevada, most crops need to be irrigated. Hay, barley, potatoes, cantaloupes, figs, and grapes are some of the state's harvests.

A cowboy on horseback rounds up a steer.

Protecting the Environment

Each year, hundreds of thousands of people move to Nevada. The Las Vegas area alone takes in about 5,000 new residents each month. Many companies, attracted partly by low taxes and inexpensive land, are making Nevada their base. Nevada is one of the fastest growing states in the nation.

Nevada is also the driest state in the country, receiving only 9 inches (23 cm) of **precipitation** (rain and melted snow) each year. This does not supply the state with enough water, so people and crops must rely on water that has been stored away.

Nevada's farmers need water to irrigate their fields *(opposite page)*. Growing cities such as Las Vegas *(top)* rely on power plants that use large amounts of water to create electricity. Nevada's young people *(bottom)* also count on a healthy water supply.

Occasionally, storm clouds hover over Nevada, but rain is scarce in the state.

Rivers are Nevada's most plentiful source of water. The Hoover Dam was built on the Colorado River to store and supply water to parts of Nevada, Colorado, and Arizona. But the amount of water

Rivers provide much of Nevada's water.

the Hoover Dam can provide to farms, homes, and businesses is limited. Each state is allowed only so much water from the dam. If Nevada needs more than its share, Nevadans must look elsewhere for water.

Thirty-three percent of the state's water comes from underneath the ground, where nature has stored it for centuries. Water collects underground when soil soaks up rain or snow. As it seeps into the ground, the water flows through cracks in rocks that lie below the surface of the earth. Over thousands of years, large pools of water, called **aquifers,** have formed underground.

Workers use drilling machinery to reach the water in aquifers.

Nevadans dig wells to pump the **groundwater** from nearby aquifers to croplands, homes, and factories. Wells have supplied tons of water to Nevada, but as more and more groundwater is used, the water level in the aquifers gets lower and lower. Someday the aquifers may dry up.

A large factory might use more water in one day than you might use in your home in a lifetime. Some factories need tons of water to cool down machinery that is hot from operating for many hours. Other factories may boil water to create steam heat. Water is also used to help make many products.

Much of this water is not lost. It is used over and over again. But as more factories open in Nevada, more water is needed.

Households also use a lot of water. Families need water to shower, flush the toilet, cook, and do laundry. Each person uses about 100 gallons (380 liters) of water a day. With a population of more than one million, Nevadans use at least 100 million gallons (380 million liters) of water a day.

As Nevada's population grows, more people will need to use the state's limited water supply. To make sure farms, households, and businesses continue to have the water they need, Nevada must either use its water more wisely or find new sources.

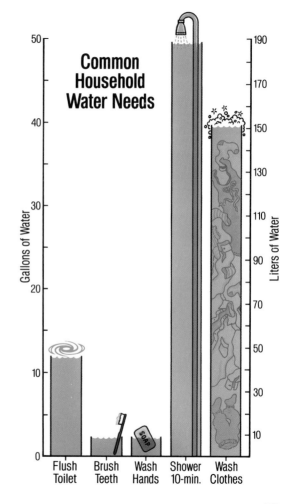

Common Household Water Needs

Gallons of Water

Liters of Water

Flush Toilet | Brush Teeth | Wash Hands | Shower 10-min. | Wash Clothes

One way to increase Nevada's water supply is to pipe or ship water in from states that have more water than they need. Some of the northern states, especially Alaska, have plenty. But shipping or piping water into Nevada would be expensive. Also, other states are not always willing to give up their water.

Although Nevadans may need to go outside their state to get more water, they can also make sure not to waste the water they do have. People can easily cut their water use by fixing leaking faucets, taking shorter showers, and sprinkling lawns less often. Factories can conserve water by using other methods to heat up or cool down machinery.

They can also use less water to make products.

By lining irrigation canals and ditches with concrete, farmers prevent water from escaping. Watertight canals also keep weeds, which drink a lot of water, from growing along the paths of the canals. Farmers can also be careful not to give the plants in their fields too much water.

More water than land covers the earth. The state of Nevada, however, has a very small fraction of the world's water supply. To meet growing needs for water, Nevadans are planning now so they will have enough water for the future.

All Nevadans, whether they live in cities (opposite page) **or in the country, can help conserve Nevada's water** (above).

61

Nevada's Famous People

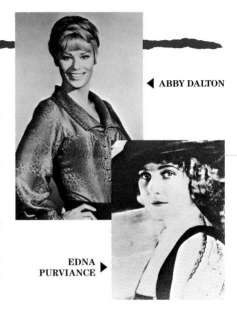

◀ ABBY DALTON

ACTORS

Ben Alexander (1911–1969) played the part of Officer Frank Smith on the television series "Dragnet" from 1953 to 1959. (He was later replaced by actor Harry Morgan, whose character was named Bill Gannon.) Alexander, who was born Nicholas Benton, was from Garfield, Nevada.

Abby Dalton (born 1935), of Las Vegas, played Julia Cumson on the television show "Falcon Crest," which was popular in the 1980s. Dalton has appeared in several other series, including "Barney Miller."

Edna Purviance (1896–1958) starred in many of Charlie Chaplin's silent movies, including *The Tramp* in 1915. Purviance was born in Paradise Valley, Nevada, and grew up in Lovelock.

EDNA ▶
PURVIANCE

◀ DAT-SO-LA-LEE

ARTIST

Dat-So-La-Lee (1835?–1925) was a Washo Indian basket weaver who lived in Carson Valley, Nevada. Some of her baskets took months to make and were worth thousands of dollars. Her art is displayed at several museums around the country, including the Nevada State Museum in Carson City.

BUSINESS LEADERS

Eva Adams (born 1908) began her career as a professor at the University of Nevada. From 1961 to 1969, she was director of

◀ EVA ADAMS

the U.S. Mint, where she supervised the making and storing of coins. Adams has also worked as a consultant, teaching supervisors how to better manage their employees.

James E. Casey (1888–1983) founded United Parcel Service (UPS) in 1907. UPS has grown to be one of the largest independent delivery services in the world. Casey was born in Candelaria, Nevada.

William P. Sharon (1821–1885) was a powerful banker who gained control of many of Nevada's wealthiest mines. He and others in Nevada's so-called "Bank Crowd" became rich quickly. In 1875 Sharon became a U.S. senator from Nevada.

Benjamin ("Bugsy") Seigel (1906–1947) was a gangster who moved to Las Vegas from New York to build the Flamingo Hotel. The hotel and casino, which cost Seigel $6 million, opened in 1946, equipped with a maze of secret escape hatches and tunnels for gangster-style getaways. A motion picture about Seigel's life, entitled *Bugsy,* was released in 1991.

◄ JAMES
CASEY

WILLIAM
▼ SHARON

◄ BUGSY
SEIGEL

PAT ▶
NIXON

FIRST LADY

Pat Nixon (born 1912), first lady from 1969 to 1974, was born Thelma Catharine Ryan on St. Patrick's Day in a mining camp in Ely, Nevada. Because of her birthday, her father nicknamed her Pat. After graduating from college, Pat became a high-school teacher. In 1940 she married Richard Nixon, who later became president of the United States. While in the White House, Pat encouraged Americans to do volunteer work.

63

MINERS

Henry Comstock (1820–1870) was in Nevada in 1859 when a group of miners found silver on land he claimed to own. He gained large shares of the deposits, which became known as the Comstock Lode.

John William Mackay (1831–1902) became rich after his crew struck a huge vein of gold and silver ore in Virginia City. The Big Bonanza, as it was called, produced more than $100 million worth of minerals for Mackay and his partners.

◀ HENRY COMSTOCK

JOHN MACKAY ▶

▼ SARAH HOPKINS

▲ WOVOKA

JACK
KRAMER ▶

NATIVE AMERICAN LEADERS

Sarah Winnemucca Hopkins (1844?–1891) was an activist for Native American rights. Hopkins also wrote several books and established schools for Indian children. She was born near Humboldt Lake.

Wovoka (1858?–1932), also known as Jack Wilson, was a Paiute Indian religious leader born in Esmeralda County, Nevada. He originated the Ghost Dance, a religion which taught that starvation, sickness, and death could be avoided if people stopped fighting. Wovoka's ideas had spread to many tribes throughout the West before ending in the late 1890s.

SPORTS FIGURES

Jack Kramer (born 1921) became a well-known tennis player in the 1940s. He won the U.S. Open in both 1946 and 1947 and won the All-England Championship at Wimbledon in 1947. Kramer is from Las Vegas.

Greg LeMond (born 1961), a professional cyclist, moved to Washoe Valley, Nevada, at the age of seven. LeMond has won the Tour de France three times and the World Professional Championship twice. In 1989 he became the fourth person to win both races in the same year.

Jerry Tarkanian (born 1930) coached the Runnin' Rebels at the University of Nevada in Las Vegas for 19 seasons and won an average of 83 percent of the games played, the highest percentage of any college basketball coach. Tarkanian began his coaching career in 1956 and retired in 1992.

▲ GREG LeMOND

WALTER CLARK ▶

◀ SAMUEL CLEMENS

WRITERS

Walter van Tilburg Clark (1909–1971) was born in Maine, but lived in Nevada when he wrote the western novels that made him famous. Two of his books, *The Ox-Bow Incident* and *Track of the Cat,* were made into movies. Clark also wrote several nonfiction books about Nevada.

Samuel L. Clemens (1835–1910) lived in Nevada in the early 1860s. He wrote for the *Territorial Enterprise,* the Virginia City newspaper on which he began using the pen name Mark Twain. *Roughing It* is a famous story the author wrote about his adventures in Nevada.

Glen Charles (born 1943) and **Les Charles** (born 1948) of Henderson, Nevada, have written and produced several successful television series, including "M*A*S*H," "Taxi," and "Cheers." Working as a team, the two brothers have won more than a dozen awards for their scripts.

▲ GLEN *(right)* and LES CHARLES

65

Facts-at-a-Glance

Nickname: Silver State
Song: "Home Means Nevada"
Motto: All for Our Country
Flower: sagebrush
Tree: single-leaf pinyon
Bird: mountain bluebird

Population: 1,201,833*
Rank in population, nationwide: 39th
Area: 110,561 sq mi (286,352 sq km)
Rank in area, nationwide: 7th
Date and ranking of statehood:
   Oct. 31, 1864, the 36th state
Capital: Carson City (40,443*)
Major cities (and populations*):
   Las Vegas (258,295), Reno (133,850),
   Henderson (64,942), Sparks (53,367),
   North Las Vegas (47,707)
U.S. senators: 2
U.S. representatives: 2
Electoral votes: 4

Places to visit: Valley of Fire State Park near Overton, Hoover Dam near Las Vegas, Fleischmann Planetarium at the University of Nevada in Reno, Lehman Caves near Baker, Rhyolite, a ghost town near Beatty

Annual events: Chariot Racing in Wells (Jan.–Feb.), Wild Bunch Stampede in Fallon (May), Pony Express Days in Ely (Aug.), International Camel Races (Sept.), Boulder City Parade of Lights on Lake Mead (Dec.)

*1990 census

66

Natural resources: copper, mercury, gold, silver, magnesite, iron ore, lead, salt, limestone, oil, sand and gravel

Agricultural products: beef, hay, alfalfa, barley, potatoes, wheat

Manufactured goods: computers, electronic components, concrete, printed materials, food products, metal products, chemicals, lumber products

ENDANGERED SPECIES

Mammals—gray wolf

Birds—peregrine falcon, bald eagle, wood stork, brown pelican, least tern

Fish—cui-ui, bonytail chub, Clover Valley speckled dace, Ash Meadows Amargosa pupfish

Plants—steamboat buckwheat, Monte Neva paint-brush, Amargosa niterwort, Sodaville milk-vetch, Ash Meadows gum plant

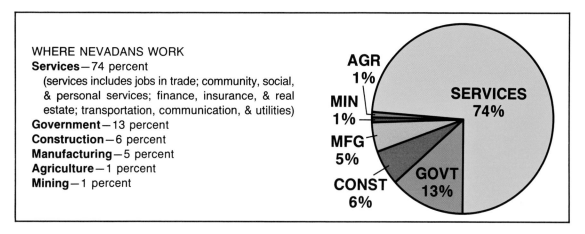

WHERE NEVADANS WORK
Services—74 percent
  (services includes jobs in trade; community, social, & personal services; finance, insurance, & real estate; transportation, communication, & utilities)
Government—13 percent
Construction—6 percent
Manufacturing—5 percent
Agriculture—1 percent
Mining—1 percent

AGR 1%
MIN 1%
MFG 5%
CONST 6%
GOVT 13%
SERVICES 74%

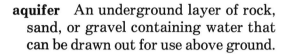
PRONUNCIATION GUIDE

Basques (BASKS)

Genoa (juh-NOH-uh)

Lahontan (luh-HAHN-tuhn)

Paiute (PY-yoot)

Pueblo (poo-EHB-loh)

Rhyolite (RY-uh-lyt)

Shoshone (shuh-SHOHN)

Sierra Nevada
   (see-EHR-uh nuh-VAD-uh)

Tahoe (TAH-hoh)

Tonopah (TOHN-uh-pah)

Winnemucca (wihn-uh-MUHK-uh)

aquifer An underground layer of rock, sand, or gravel containing water that can be drawn out for use above ground.

casino A room or building where people gamble.

desert An area of land that receives only about 10 inches (25 cm) or less of rain or snow a year. Some deserts are mountainous; others are expanses of rock, sand, or salt flats.

flash flood A sudden, short-lived flood that usually occurs after a heavy rain.

gambling Placing bets (usually money) on a game such as poker or dice.

ghost town A town that was once booming but has since been deserted because a natural resource such as gold or silver has been used up.

groundwater Water that lies beneath the earth's surface. The water comes from rain and snow that seep through soil into the cracks and other openings in rocks. Groundwater supplies wells and springs.

immigrant A person who moves into a foreign country and settles there.

irrigation A method of watering land by directing water through canals, ditches, pipes, or sprinklers.

lava Hot, melted rock that erupts from a volcano or from cracks in the earth's surface and that hardens as it cools.

mesa An isolated hill with steep sides and a flat top.

plateau A large, relatively flat area that stands above the surrounding land.

precipitation Rain, snow, hail, and other forms of moisture that fall to earth.

pueblo Any of the ancient Indian villages in the southwestern United States with buildings of stone or clay, usually built one above the other. The word *Pueblo* also refers to an Indian tribe that lives in the Southwest.

reservation Public land set aside by the government to be used by Native Americans.

reservoir A place where water is collected and stored for later use.

rural Having to do with the countryside or farming.

Index ━━━━━━━━━━━━━━━━━━━━━━━━━━━━━━━━━━▶

Acknowledgments:

Maryland Cartographics, Inc., pp. 2, 10; Kent & Donna Dannen, pp. 2-3, 8-9, 42, 48, 56; Jack Lindstrom, p. 6; Patrick Cone, pp. 7, 8 (left), 19, 51, 52; David Matherly/Visuals Unlimited, pp. 11, 12; Lake Tahoe Visitors Authority, pp. 13, 50 (top); James Blank/Root Resources, p. 14; Doyen Salsig, pp. 15, 16, 18, 32, 44, 58; Anthony Mercieca/Root Resources, p. 17; *Pine Tree Ceremonial Dance,* by José Rey Toledos, University of Oklahoma Museum of Art, Norman, Oklahoma, p. 21; Pueblo Grande de Nevada Collection, University of Nevada, Las Vegas Library, Spec. Coll. Neg. #0143 0484, p. 22; Nevada Historical Society, pp. 25, 26-27, 27 (right), 28, 30, 33, 62 (top right, bottom left), 64 (center left); W. H. Shockley Collection, University of Nevada, Las Vegas Library, Spec. Coll. Neg. #0241 0002, p. 31; Special Collections, University of Nevada—Reno Library, pp. 34, 63 (center right), 65 (top right); National Archives, p. 35; Gladys Frazier Collection, University of Nevada, Las Vegas Library, Spec. Coll. Neg. #0039 0006, p. 36; Library of Congress, p. 37; Las Vegas News Bureau, pp. 38, 55 (top); Mystic Stamp Company, p. 39; Jeff Greenberg, pp. 41, 45 (right), 50 (bottom), 53, 55 (bottom); Nevada Commission on Tourism, p. 45 (left); Department of General Services, p. 46; Circus Circus Hotel/Casino—Las Vegas, Pro Process-Pro Display, p. 47; National Park Service, p. 49; Nevada Division of Water Planning, pp. 54, 57, 61; Bruce Berg/Visuals Unlimited, p. 60; Hollywood Book & Poster Co., p. 62 (top left); UNLV Collection, University of Nevada, Las Vegas Library, p. 62 (bottom right); United Parcel Service, p. 63 (top); Flamingo Hilton, p. 63 (center left); Nixon Presidential Materials Project, p. 63 (bottom); *Dictionary of American Portraits,* pp. 64 (top left, top right), 65 (center); Bureau of American Ethnology Collection, National Anthropological Archives, Smithsonian Institution, p. 64 (center right); International Tennis Hall of Fame and Tennis Museum at the Newport Casino, Newport, Rhode Island, p. 64 (bottom); Kiefel Sportfolio, p. 65 (top left); Cheers, p. 65 (bottom); Jean Matheny, p. 66; Darren Erickson. p. 69; Skylar Hansen, p. 71.